Gus Loses a Tooth

SCHOLASTIC READER
PRE
LEVEL
1
30-100 WORDS

Gus Loses a Tooth

by Frank Remkiewicz

SCHOLASTIC INC.

For Paul Jaworski and
all the great smile-crafters
at thirty-nine ninety

Copyright © 2013 by Frank Remkiewicz

All rights reserved. Published by Scholastic Inc.
SCHOLASTIC and associated logos are
trademarks and/or registered trademarks of Scholastic Inc.
Lexile is a registered trademark of MetaMetrics, Inc.

ISBN 978-0-545-46911-1

12 11 10 9 8 7 6 5   14 15 16 17 18/0

Printed in the U.S.A.   40
First printing, January 2013

This tooth is loose.

Look!

Gus shows his friends.

They all want one, too.

Gus needs a check-up.

This tooth *is* loose.

It will fall out soon.

And the next day . . .

. . . it did.

Look, Mom!

Look, Dad!

Look, Goldy!

Gus has a plan.

Time for bed.

What was that?

It must be the Tooth Fairy.

Gus is rich!

Thanks, Tooth Fairy.

Gus has a new plan.

Smile, Gus!